W9-AVM-087

A Beginning-to-Read Book

THE BALL BOOK

by Margaret Hillert

Illustrated by Nan Brooks

NORWOOD **H**OUSE 🏠 **P**RESS

DEAR CAREGIVER,

The *Beginning-to-Read* series is a carefully written collection of classic readers you may remember from your own childhood. Each book features text comprised of common sight words to provide your child ample practice reading the words that appear most frequently in written text. The many additional details in the pictures enhance the story and offer the opportunity for you to help your child expand oral language and develop comprehension.

Begin by reading the story to your child, followed by letting him or her read familiar words and soon your child will be able to read the story independently. At each step of the way, be sure to praise your reader's efforts to build his or her confidence as an independent reader. Discuss the pictures and encourage your child to make connections between the story and his or her own life. At the end of the story, you will find reading activities and a word list that will help your child practice and strengthen beginning reading skills.

Above all, the most important part of the reading experience is to have fun and enjoy it!

Shannon Cannon

Shannon Cannon,
Literacy Consultant

Norwood House Press • P.O. Box 316598 • Chicago, Illinois 60631
For more information about Norwood House Press please visit our website at *www.norwoodhousepress.com* or call 866-565-2900.

LIBRARY OF CONGRESS CATALOGING-IN-PUBLICATION DATA

Hillert, Margaret.
  The ball book / by Margaret Hillert ; illustrated by Nan Brooks.
    p. cm. — (Beginning to read series. Easy stories)
    Summary: People play a variety of games involving balls on the big ball that is Earth. Includes reading activities.
    ISBN-13: 978-1-59953-031-4 (library edition : alk. paper)
    ISBN-10: 1-59953-031-7 (library edition : alk. paper)
    [1. Ball games—Fiction. 2. Balls (Sporting goods)—Fiction. 3.Games—Fiction. 4. Readers.] I. Brooks, Nan, ill. II. Title. III. Series.
    PZ7.H558Bal 2006
    [E]—dc22   2005033392

Balls, balls, balls.
Big balls. Little balls.
Balls for you and me.

I like balls.
I can play with this one.
I make it go up and down.

You can play with me.
Look out.
Here it comes.
Get it. Get it.

This is fun to play.
The ball is a little one.
Can you get this little ball?

Look at the little ones here.
Pretty little ones.
Make one go in.
Make one go out.

Here is a big ball.
You can jump on it.
Jump, jump, jump.

And here is one for the cat.
Something is in this little ball.
The cat will run and run to
get it.

This is a little ball, too.
I make it go.

You make it go.
We have fun with it.

You have to get this ball up.
Up, up, and in.
You have to work at it.
Work, work, work.

Now look at this ball.
You can make something go
down with it.
Down, down, down.

Good, good.
You did it!

You did it!
Good for you.

And this is fun, too.

You have to run, run, run
to get this ball.
Oh, my. Oh, my.

Father and Mother like to
play with this ball.

Look at it go.
Away, away it goes.

Look up, up, up.

Get this ball up.
Help it go.

This is good to play at school.
But you have to look out!
Look out for this ball.

Here is a funny ball.
Can you guess what it is for?
What can you do with it?

This is what you
do with it.
You run and run
and run.

We can play with this ball,
and we see it on TV.
We run and run with
this ball, too.

This ball is fun to play with.
You are good at this.
Mother and Father come to
see you play.

This is a big, big, BIG ball!
We are on this ball.
That is funny.

We work on it.
We play on it.

What a good ball it is!

READING REINFORCEMENT

The following activities support the findings of the National Reading Panel that determined the most effective components for reading instruction are: Phonemic Awareness, Phonics, Vocabulary, Fluency, and Text Comprehension.

Phonemic Awareness:
The Phonograms –all and -ook
Oral Blending: Say the beginning and ending parts of the following words and ask your child to listen to the sounds and say the whole word:

/b/ + all = ball	/f/ + all = fall	/t/ + all = tall
/w/ + all = wall	/m/ + all = mall	/h/ + all = hall
/b/ + ook = book	/l/ + ook = look	/c/ + ook = cook
/t/ + ook = took	/h/ + ook = hook	/n/ + ook = nook

Phonics: The letters b, c, f, h, l, m, n, t

1. Fold a piece of paper in half down the middle. Draw a line on the fold.

2. At the top of the paper, to the left of the line, write the phonogram _**all**.

3. At the top of the paper, to the right of the line, write the phonogram _**ook**.

4. Write the letters **b, c, f, h, l, m, n, t** on small pieces of paper.

5. Using the letters, ask your child to make as many **–all** and **–ook** words as he or she can and to write those words in the correct column.

Vocabulary: Adjectives

1. Explain to your child that words that describe something are called adjectives.

2. Say the following adjectives and ask your child to name something that the adjective might describe:

| cold | pretty | huge | fast | hot | scratchy |
| soft | loud | tiny | slow | funny | delicious |

3. Explain to your child that adjectives can sometimes describe a type of something. The story is about many different kinds of balls.

4. Ask your child to name the different kinds of balls in the story. Write the words that describe the kinds of balls in the story on sticky note paper.

5. Mix the words up and randomly say each word to your child. Ask your child to point to the correct word.

6. Ask your child to place the sticky notes on the pages in the book where the adjective describes the kind of ball on that page.

Fluency: Shared Reading

1. Reread the story to your child at least two more times while your child tracks the print by running a finger under the words as they are read. Ask your child to read the words he or she knows with you.

2. Reread the story taking turns, alternating readers between sentences or pages.

Text Comprehension: Discussion Time

1. Ask your child to retell the sequence of events in the story.

2. To check comprehension, ask your child the following questions:

   • What kinds of ball games can you play with one friend?

   • What kind of ball games can you play with many friends or on a team?

   • Why do you think the author says we live on a ball?

   • What is your favorite ball game? Why?

The Ball Book uses the 62 words listed below.

This list can be used to practice reading the words that appear in the text.
You may wish to write the words on index cards and use them to help your
child build automatic word recognition. Regular practice with these words
will enhance your child's fluency in reading connected text.

a	Father	I	oh	that
and	for	in	on	the
are	fun	is	one (s)	this
at	funny	it	out	to
away				too
	get	jump	play	TV
ball (s)	go		pretty	
big	goes	like		up
but	good	little	run	
	guess	look		we
can			school	what
cat	have	make	see	will
come (s)	help	me	something	with
	here	Mother		work
did		my		
do				you
down		now		

ABOUT THE AUTHOR Margaret Hillert has written over 80 books for
children who are just learning to read. Her books
have been translated into many different languages and over a million children
throughout the world have read her books. She first started writing poetry as
a child and has continued to write for children and adults throughout her life. A
first grade teacher for 34 years, Margaret is now retired from teaching and lives in
Michigan where she likes to write, take walks in the morning, and care for her three cats.

Photograph by Glenna Washburn

ABOUT THE ADVISER Shannon Cannon contributed the activities pages that appear in
this book. Shannon serves as a literacy consultant and provides
staff development to help improve reading instruction. She is a frequent presenter at educational
conferences and workshops. Prior to this she worked as an elementary school teacher and as
president of a curriculum publishing company.